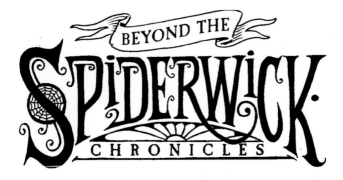

"They're faeries! They're tricking us!"

BEYOND THE
SPIDERWICK
CHRONICLES

THE NIXIE'S SONG
BOOK ONE OF THREE

Tony DiTerlizzi and Holly Black

Simon and Schuster Books for Young Readers
New York   London   Toronto   Sydney

SIMON & SCHUSTER BOOKS FOR YOUNG READERS
An imprint of Simon & Schuster Children's Publishing Division
1230 Avenue of the Americas, New York, New York 10020

10 9 8 7 6 5 4

CIP data for this book is available from the Library of Congress.
ISBN-13: 978-0-689-87131-3 • ISBN-10: 0-689-87131-7

To my grandfather, Harry,
who liked to make up stories.
—H. B.

To all my friends and family back in Florida.
These images of my old home are for you.
—T. D.

Storied old New England is
where this vast tale was born.
Three kids, an antique house, a book,
a dad from daughter torn,

an unexpected escapade
into a tricksy land—
with dangers unpredictable
so very close at hand.

The kids were tested fearless.
The book was lost then found.
The dad was reunited then
passed on without a sound.

Evil was soundly thwarted
like in fairy tales of old,
but there's no happy ending.
No! Because the tale was told . . .

. . . to Tony DiTerlizzi and
his partner, Holly Black.
They took the story coast to coast,
around the globe, and back.

Then that pair took the secrets
and put them into a book,
a guide to the fantastical
for all who cared to look.

Now each and every single day
the story grows and roves.
It wanders beneath maples, birches,
pines, and old mangroves.

So when you walk among the trees,
look close and do not blink,
because the world you're entering
is
BIGGER
THAN YOU THINK.

Table of Contents

List of Full-Page Illustrations

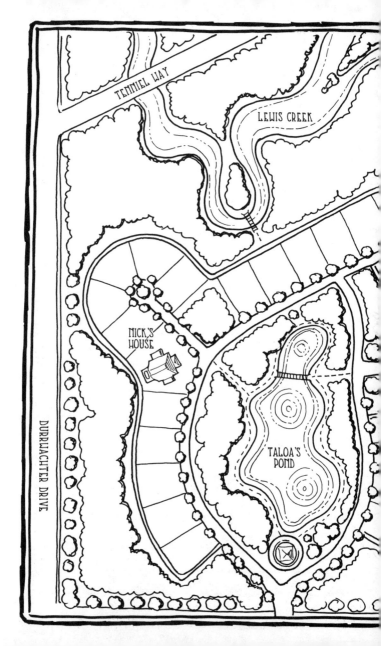

To
Jack's House

WETLAND
PRESERVE

RECREATION
AREA

MANGROVE HOLLOW

"A COMMUNITY SET IN NAT

"What are you thinking about?"

Chapter One

IN WHICH There Are Many Different Sorts of Developments

After his mother died, Nicholas Vargas stopped bothering. His Aunt Armena had told him to be good and not to bother his father, but he decided that her advice could extend to everyone and everything. It seemed that Nick's brother had the same idea—Jules never hung around long enough to bother anyone anymore. So the whole family kept on not bothering each other right up until Nick and Jules's dad suddenly decided to get married again.

Leading his new stepsister up the carpeted

NICK VARGAS

stairs, Nick had to keep his jaw clenched to stop himself from shouting. He hated that he had to give up his room and move in with Jules, who snored all night and woke up at the crack of dawn to go surfing. If his father hadn't married his stepmother after only six months of dating, Nick would still have his own room. And he wouldn't be stuck with a bedroom-stealing stepsister. Laurie was almost exactly his age and the biggest, weirdest loser he'd ever met. She bothered everyone.

Nick thought he was being fair about it, too, because he'd been called a loser and a nerd and a spaz himself. He was eleven, kind of fat, and bad at sports, while Julian shredded waves and made it to state in track. The only thing Nick thought *he* was really good at was school, and that was mostly about being quiet and following directions. So, okay, he knew he wasn't cool. At least he knew better than to advertise everything lame about himself. Laurie seemed to be proud to be the lamest person alive.

LAURIE VARGAS

"What are you thinking about?" Laurie asked him, hugging a box to her chest. Her skirt brushed the floor, making the little bells along the hem jingle.

Nick cringed and set down another box of her crap on the canopy bed. All the boxes seemed to be labeled UNICORNS, FAIRIES, or BOOKS ABOUT UNICORNS AND FAIRIES. A few of them had even bled glitter onto the hall rug.

"Things I hate," said Nick.

"Like what?" Laurie tucked a tangle of blond hair behind her ear. Bracelets clattered at her wrists.

He was tempted to tell her. "Clowns," he said instead. "They creep me out."

"I hate my name," she told him, like he'd just given her the green light to overshare. "I wish I was called Lauranathana."

"That's stupid," said Nick. "Everyone would make fun of you."

"I don't care what people think," Laurie said simply, like she meant it.

He wanted to snap at her, to tell her that *everyone* cared what people thought about them, but his dad had told him to be "civil" on moving day. He sighed. "Okay, so what stuff do you *like*?"

He looked out of her window at the empty concrete shells of houses going up all around theirs. When it had been his window, he'd liked to watch as workers poured and smoothed foundations and cut planks and nailed them in place. He liked to smell the sawdust and see that his dad's development was finally, really happening. Even though there was still some swampy forest left, soon it would all be cut back and turned into golf courses, swimming pools, and lots of other cool things. Stuff *he* liked.

He'd imagined playing out there with other kids, but the construction was behind schedule.

"A field guide."

Nothing was done. His dad kept complaining about the weather—it was the hottest summer he could remember. And that, along with the brushfires and water rationing, had everyone on edge. The sun had turned the grass on the front lawn crunchy and brown, and Nicholas's dad hadn't filled the pool in the backyard, even though he usually filled the pools as soon as they were built. Now, with the rainy season about to start, Nick's whole summer was turning out to be as lame as his stepsister.

"I like all this stuff, I guess." Laurie stacked books onto her white beadboard shelves. They were mostly fantasy and fairy tales, but she'd set aside a big tome that had gold letters and what looked like a hawk on the cover.

"What's that?" he asked.

"A field guide. So you can tell which kind of faeries are which. I bet there are a lot around here, since there's so much nature."

"You don't really believe in that stuff, do you?" He took the book from her and flipped through it. It was filled with paintings and sketches of things that made the hair along his arms stand up. They didn't look like faeries. He flipped to the back. "This isn't some kind of ancient magical text. It's fake. It was published in 2005 in New York."

"It's a reprint," Laurie told him.

"Look," he said, turning the book toward her. "It says 'fiction' inside. Explain that."

"They had to put that there," Laurie said, taking it out of his hands. "So they don't get in trouble or sued. And if you don't believe me, you can ask the authors yourself, since they're signing—"

"Hey, kids," Nick's father called from downstairs in that new, cheerful voice he used around Laurie and Charlene. "Lunch!"

After Nick and Julian's mom died and before their dad decided he needed to impress Charlene and her wacko daughter, lunch had been cold slices of leftover pizza from the night before or, on at least one occasion, a piece of apple pie with cheese melted on it. Now, apparently, it was alphabet soup and bologna sandwiches. With the crusts cut off. Nick wanted to hurl.

Downstairs in the kitchen, Julian was already sitting at the granite island. Earbud cords hung from his head, and his thumbs jabbed at the game console cradled in his hands. His hair was stiff with salt. He didn't even look up when Nick sat down next to him.

Laurie still had the stupid book tucked under one arm. "After lunch, I'm going to go look for faeries," she told her mother.

Charlene smiled mildly. "Maybe Nick can go with you. Show you around the neighborhood."

Nick scowled at his soup. Charlene was okay, but he wished she wasn't around all the time. And he wished she would stop trying to make him be friends with her daughter. Although Charlene hadn't seemed to figure it out yet, he was willing to ignore them if they'd just ignore him back.

Laurie took a bowl and crumbled a handful of Goldfish crackers into it, making a mess. It never seemed to matter what Laurie did or how bothersome she was. No one was going to tell her to stop.

"Faeries," Nick's dad said with a grin, tucking a paper napkin into his collar. "I thought they were only in England. Down here, the palmetto bugs'll get them if the lizards don't."

Nick snickered.

"They're not all small, you know," said Laurie. She clearly didn't think his dad's joke was funny, which, in Nick's opinion, only made it funnier.

"It's too hot to look for anything," Nick said, smiling down at his reflection in the granite. "Especially things that don't exist."

Nick's dad frowned and then rubbed the bridge of his nose. Maybe he was upset his joke hadn't gone over all that well. "Go help her look. Keep her from getting lost."

Nick pushed the noodle letters in his soup so they spelled L-A-M-E. Lame. Like his summer. Like his stepsister. Like how he felt as he slurped his soup down and, without saying a thing, followed Laurie out into the yard.

"What are you doing?"

Chapter Two

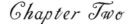

IN WHICH Nicholas Goes for an Ill-Fated Walk

With that weird book tucked under one arm, Laurie walked around the hot, fresh-poured asphalt streets like she was on some kind of exciting safari. She tried to peer into the partially finished houses. She looked behind buildings as Nick grudgingly trailed along. Laurie stopped at the newly made lake, with grates under each of the bridges to keep alligators out and a fountain in the middle that kept it from going stagnant, and then kicked off her flip-flops.

"What are you doing?" Nick asked her. He wondered how long he had to follow her around. He wondered if you could die from boredom.

She tied her long skirt up high on her legs. "Wading."

"I thought we were looking for faeries," he said, glancing back at his house. The kitchen window had a pretty good view of the lake, so pushing her in was out of the question.

"I am," she said. "I'm checking for hoofprints on the bank. That would be evidence that a kelpie lives here. Or maybe I'll find reed pipes made by nixies."

"What's a kelpie?"

"A water horse." She dragged one bare foot through the silt and made her voice ominous. "It tricks people into getting onto its back and then drowns them. Spooky, right?"

"Whatever. Why would you want to find that?"

"I know better than to ride it," she said. "I'm not stupid. The Guide tells you how to handle faeries."

Nick sighed and scrunched his toes against the fronts of his sneakers. He wouldn't have minded going in the brackish water, but his dad would freak. He didn't want Nick swimming in anything that wasn't full of chlorine and was always giving dire warnings about jellyfish and riptides to Jules. "You're not going to find anything, you know. Nothing lives here, except maybe turtles. They just dredged this lake. They're going to dump in some fish eventually, but no one's got around to it yet."

Laurie kicked over an empty turtle shell. "I guess a turtle *used* to live here. Looks like something got it." She padded over to where the tangles of fresh-planted sea grapes met the old woods. There, pinwheel-like palms grew beside the puffy tufts of pine trees. "You must come out here all the time with Jules. You're so lucky to have a brother to do stuff with."

"Yeah," Nick said. He didn't feel like explaining that Jules was busy a lot with his friends and his girlfriend. It was none of her business.

"I always wished I had a brother."

The air was hot and thick and sticky. Nick thought longingly of the air-conditioning and the games in his bedroom. Then he remembered his bedroom wasn't his bedroom anymore. No longer his territory. "We're not allowed to walk in the woods."

"We won't go far," she said, opening the book and holding it out as she picked her way through the scrub, leaving the water and Nick behind. "Be on the lookout for strange footprints or boulders that look like they have eyes. Or trees

with eyes. Or anything with eyes. And especially look to see if you find a four-leaf clover or a stone that has a hole worn through it."

"Don't be so dumb," said Nick, looking at the empty turtle shell. "I've never seen anything like that."

Laurie didn't answer. She just kept going. As he followed, he caught glimpses of her between palm trees and scrub. The distant sounds of construction served only to remind him of how far they were from anyone. A storm was coming. In the dim light, the leaves had turned silvery and strange.

"This is boring," Nick said halfheartedly.

Laurie shrugged, her flip-flop straps threaded through her fingers, her bare feet crushing reindeer moss as she got deeper into the woods. He didn't want to continue following her, but he didn't want to be standing all by himself like an idiot, either.

"Have you ever found one?" Nick called, walking through shrubs that caught on the fabric of his shorts. He pulled himself free.

"One what?" She was only a few feet away, looking closely at the side of a palm tree. It was grooved with shallow woodpecker holes.

Nick jogged over and then wheezed, already out of breath. "Something out of the book."

Laurie frowned. "I don't know," she said finally. Sandspurs had scratched thin lines on her calves, but she didn't even seem to notice. "I guess I've seen some weird stuff—like, look at the way the hill slopes over there."

Nick squinted. He'd never been even this far in the woods, and he wasn't sure what he was supposed to be noticing about the hill that was even farther on, but it was true that on the hill, long banyan-tree roots grew like a beard beside a strange-shaped boulder that resembled a sleeping eye. He shuddered. Either Laurie's crazy was contagious or he was getting heatstroke.

Looking down at his feet, Nick realized he was standing in a patch of clover. He glanced over at his stepsister, but she hadn't noticed, so he squatted down and ran his fingers through the green plants.

Just as Nick was going to straighten up, he saw a single four-leaf clover. He reached out and carefully pinched it off at the stem. If he

gave it to Laurie, he bet that she'd agree to go back to the house, but he'd never found one before and he wasn't sure he wanted to give it up. He twirled it once in his fingers. Somehow it suddenly seemed greener, more vivid, as though his vision had sharpened. Maybe the clover would make him lucky, and some other kid would move in to one of the houses and save him from a summer with Laurie.

Searching through his pockets, he came up with a receipt that looked like it had been through the laundry once. He folded the clover inside it and tucked it back in his shorts.

Laurie squeaked, and he looked over at her guiltily. She was looking up. Rain splashed on Nick in fat, warm drops.

"Summer storm," he said. "Let's go back!"

But Laurie, freak that she was, just lifted her hands and spun around as her hair plastered her neck and her skirt got soaked. "Come on, Nick," she said. "Let's pretend that we're tree spirits!"

That was the final straw for Nicholas. He didn't care if his dad yelled at him for leaving Laurie by herself. He didn't care if she couldn't find her way back and got lost in the woods and an alligator ate her. He was going home and playing his video games, and that was that. Turning his back to her, he started walking.

He followed the lake around, listening to the raindrops hiss as they hit asphalt. The rain stopped as Nick stepped onto his own scraggly, brown lawn. He sighed. It hadn't rained long enough to really make a difference, just enough to annoy him. He walked in the door and went up to his room, where there were games he knew how to win.

Lightning cracked, shooting horizontally through the sky, and thunder boomed. The rain hadn't started up again, but it sounded like it was going to come down hard when the storm blew all the way in. Nick concentrated. If he just collected a couple more mushrooms, he could give them to the old wise woman and collect the Blade of Ultimates.

Suddenly, the room went black and his screen powered off before he could save or do anything but stare dumbly. He scrambled up off the beanbag in his new, shared bedroom. Downstairs, he heard his father's voice but not what his father said. The lightning flashed again and, through the bedroom window, Nicholas saw a pale body out on the wide stretch of grass between the lake and the remaining wetlands.

He squinted. Laurie. He couldn't remember how long it had been since he came inside, and he wasn't sure if the sky had gotten dark because it was late or because of the storm. But if that was Laurie on the grass, why was she just lying there? What could have —?

His mind shied away from completing the thought.

Nicholas saw a pale body.

After scrambling down the stairs, he ran out the back door. The lack of rain was a rippling, oppressive pressure in the air. The streetlights weren't on, but flashes of lightning turned the sky bright enough for Nick to see. He ran as fast as he could toward the body before everything went black again. Then he kept running through the dark, only to stop suddenly as he got close. He choked on a scream.

A creature lay on its side—its green skin fading to white in places and dry as a leaf. Its eyes were closed and it didn't seem to have a nose—just two slits above a slash of a mouth. Weird tendrils stuck up from the creature's forehead, and brownish ribbons of grass covered its head like hair.

It wasn't covered in purple glitter.

It didn't have wings.

But Nicholas had a sinking feeling that it was going to turn out to be a faerie anyway.

He took a deep breath and pushed.

Chapter Three

IN WHICH Nicholas Lifts
More Than an Eyebrow

L aurie," Nick said breathlessly, opening the door to his old bedroom. She was lying on her stomach on the bed, with her clarinet in one hand and a book of music open in front of her. The fan turned lazily overhead. New posters were taped up on the walls.

"There's something out there," he told her, trying to keep his voice from trembling. "One of your stupid monsters."

"You didn't knock." She frowned.

Nick sputtered. "It's *my* room! Just because

you're in it doesn't make it yours. I don't have to knock on the door to *my* room!"

"I'm telling your dad!" she yelled.

"Fine!" Nick banged his knuckles against the wall. "Happy? I knocked!"

"You just left me out there without saying anything. I looked for you for*ever*."

"Laurie!" he shouted. "Shut up and listen!"

Her eyes went wide and her nostrils flared, but she pressed her lips flat.

"There's a thing out there!" Nick could feel himself shaking as he pointed to the window.

Laurie got off the bed slowly and stuck her feet in her purple flip-flops. "Okay. Fine. Show me."

He pointed out the window toward the pale body. Laurie shook her head even though she was so close to the glass that her forehead was pressed against it.

"It's the whitish thing," Nick said.

Laurie put her hand on her hip. "There's nothing there."

"I'll show you up close," he said.

"You want me to go outside? Now?"

Nick groaned in frustration. *"Please."*

He led her downstairs and through the grass to the creature, pulling her to a stop when they got close. It didn't seem as though it had moved. He wondered if it was dead. He wondered if they should donate it to a museum. "See?" he said.

If they did donate it to a museum, the plaque would say that he'd found it. Maybe they'd name it after him. Vargas's whatever-it-was.

"Ha ha," Laurie said, turning back to the house. "Stop making fun of me."

"What?" Nick asked. "Can't you see it?"

"Of course I can't see it, jerk. There's nothing there."

He opened his mouth and closed it again, too stunned to know what to say. Then he realized she was going to leave him alone with the creature. "Wait!" he called after her. "Wait! Laurie, I swear it's real. Look! It's right there and green and really creepy and I promise I'm not making this up."

She turned around and looked at him for a long moment. "I don't understand." She pushed her glasses up higher on the bridge of her nose. "You're serious? How can you see something I don't? You have the Sight? That's so not fair."

"No kidding," Nick said.

"You're not the seventh son of a seventh son. You don't have red hair. How did you get it?" She stopped. "Did anyone spit in your eye recently?"

"That's gross," he said. "No way."

She narrowed her eyes, and Nick suddenly thought she was going to forget her rainbow-y happy crap and strangle him.

"Well," he said. "I did find one of those clovers you were looking for."

"You found a *four-leaf clover*?"

He shrugged. "You mean, that's why I can see it?"

"Of course." She put her hand on her hip. "Give it here. Four-leaf clovers let you see faeries, you idiot!"

He reached into the pocket of his cargo shorts and carefully pulled out and unfolded the paper where he'd kept the plant. It was wilted at the edges but otherwise okay. Laurie held her breath as she carefully undid the string from around her neck and slid off her locket, thumbing it open. Charlene's picture was on one side and a bearded guy that Nick guessed was Laurie's dad was on the other. She put the clover over her mother's head and closed the locket around it.

"*Oh,*" she said softly, her voice full of surprised rapture as she squeezed the locket in her palm. Nick's vision faded to normal. The night seemed darker, less vivid. He told himself that he was relieved not to have to see the creature anymore before he realized he wouldn't know if it moved. That sent a shiver of dread through him.

It creeped him out that the thing even *existed*.

Laurie bent down, eyes wide and shining. "She's a nixie, I think. She must have left her pond and not been able to make it back."

Nick thought of the dried husks of toads he sometimes saw on the newly paved roads. "Is it dead?"

Laurie reached out and stroked just above the grass, like she was petting the thing, smoothing its hair. Nick shuddered and took a step back. Thunder boomed overhead, but more rain still refused to fall.

"I don't think so," she said. "Her heart's beating."

"Good. Fine. If it's alive, then let's leave it," Nick said, but he was afraid Laurie wasn't going

"Get a wheelbarrow."

to be persuaded to go back to the house that easily. "Dinner's probably going to be ready soon. They'll start looking for us."

"Get a wheelbarrow," Laurie told him. "We have to put her back in the lake."

"You're not supposed to touch wild animals when they're sick. They could attack you. They could be rabid."

"She's not a wild animal. She's a *faerie*."

"Fine." When he'd gone back to get Laurie, this was what he'd been hoping—that she'd tell him what this thing was and what they should do with it. But walking across the construction site in the dark was far more frightening than it had been hours ago, when the only things he'd been afraid of were stepping on a water moccasin or banana spiders dropping on his face.

Now he wasn't sure what to be afraid of. He grabbed the handles of the wheelbarrow and tugged it out of a pile of dirt. As he was steering it back toward Laurie and the creature, his father opened the door to their house.

"Nicholas!" he yelled. "What are you doing? Leave that alone!"

Nick looked up. He never got in trouble. Never. He hated Laurie. She'd changed everything when she showed up.

"Get in here," he said. "Dinner's been ready for half an hour. We were calling you. Where's your stepsister?"

"I'll go get her," Nick said.

When the door closed, he took a deep breath and pushed the wheelbarrow as fast as he could. He knew his father was disappointed in him. Disappointed, which was much worse than mad.

"Laurie," he said when he got to her. "We have to go in. Dad's calling us for dinner."

"This is important," said Laurie. "Please. I can't carry her by myself."

Nick shook his head. "We can sneak out after."

"She could die," Laurie said softly.

Nick thought of his mother, who did die. He didn't want to cause anything's death. Even this thing's.

"Okay," said Nick. "But we have to be quick."

"Grab her feet." Laurie reached down and seemed to lift something. Nick gritted his teeth and touched where he thought the nixie was. Under his fingers, her skin was dry as paper. When he looked down, he saw her with the same vivid, strange vision as when he had held the clover. His heart beat so loudly he thought he could hear it. He slid his hands up to her ankles and couldn't help feeling her webbed feet. He had to force himself not to drop them.

The creature lifted easily.

"Okay," Nick said.

He heaved and was surprised to find that the creature lifted easily, despite it being about as tall as Laurie was. They shuffled a little and lowered it over the wheelbarrow.

"Is she in there?" Nick asked, backing away.

Laurie nodded. Nick forced himself to grab hold of the handles and push the wheelbarrow carefully toward the lake.

"Nick!" Julian called from the house. "Laurie! Get in here! Dad's been looking for you!"

Nicholas bit his lip and helped Laurie lift the nixie, then wade out and drop her in a deep enough part of the lake for her body to go under. As soon as his fingers left her skin, the Sight was gone, but he saw the water displace when she slid into it.

"Won't she drown?" he whispered.

Laurie shook her head. "They can breathe water."

For a moment the ripples seemed to still, and then the water thrashed and both of them jumped.

"What happened?" Nick asked shakily.

Laurie was smiling hugely. "She swam away! She's okay! We saved her!"

"Nicholas!" his father shouted from the doorway. He stepped out into the yard. "Didn't I tell you not to mess with that wheelbarrow!"

"Sorry, Dad," Nick said.

"Don't give me that crap. You looked right at me and lied. Now get in the house!"

"Dad, I—"

"I don't understand what's the matter with you! Are you trying to show off for Laurie?"

"No!"

"I thought you had more sense; you always

acted like you had more sense! Go eat your dinner and then get up to your room. No TV, no video games, no nothing for a week. And if you touch another piece of equipment, you'll spend the whole summer in that room!"

Nick's face felt hot as he walked into the house. His eyes stung. Nick's father said nothing to Laurie, and when they sat down at the table, Charlene didn't say anything either. They all ate in miserable silence.

As he lifted the fork to his mouth, Nick looked out at the lake and wondered if there were more creatures like that nixie, with froggy hands and feet, watching him invisibly from the shadows. He was glad that he couldn't see them. He only wished they couldn't see him either.

She sang the words.

Chapter Four

IN WHICH Nicholas Sees for the Second Time

It was hard for Nick to work on his model boat with Jules's dirty clothes and surfing magazines covering the floor and thrown across the dressers, not to mention Julian himself slumped on the bed with his earbuds in, but Nick had cleared a space on their shared "homework desk" and covered it with newspaper. He was assembling a model of a Viking ship, and he planned on attaching a motor to the bottom so it could really move. As he pictured it revving

across the lake, he kept imagining green, webbed hands reaching up to pull it down.

Thoughts of those hands had kept him up the night before. Even the light snoring of Jules on the other side of the room hadn't been reassuring. Outside, the rain had come down in sheets, and he pictured amphibious things moving through it and peeking through the windows, their finger pads sticking to the glass. He'd tossed and turned in his bed until the light showed on the horizon. Only then had he finally collapsed into sleep, which caused him to wake up late—which meant that today the dark would come even sooner, making him jittery all over again.

Earlier that afternoon, when Laurie was out with Charlene getting keys made, Nick had snuck into his old room and looked through Laurie's field guide. According to the book, nixies didn't eat people—although there seemed to be plenty of other creatures that might.

As he'd stood in the middle of the room with the Guide, looking around at the map of Narnia tacked up on his old wall, noticing Laurie's stuffed animals spread out on the bed and her junk cluttering the counter of his bathroom, he'd been overwhelmed by the suffocating desire to smash all of it. This was his room. His house. His family. Laurie and Charlene didn't belong. But all he'd done was drop the field guide and walk, trembling with rage, back to his desk.

Now he tried to attach another oar with a drop of glue, to concentrate on that activity and not on Laurie and his bedroom or the hideous creatures in the Guide or on the trolls and goblins and dragons that could be crawling around the development.

A knock on the door made Nick's fingers twitch with surprise. He snapped the thin piece of wood in his hands.

Laurie peeked her head in. "I've been talking to Taloa, and she explained that—"

"Taloa?" he asked, hoping that she meant another kid and not some not-nearly-imaginary-enough friend. He looked over at Jules, but he was flipping through a car magazine and nodding his head in time with music they couldn't hear.

"The nixie," Laurie said, and Nick felt his stomach twist.

"Don't tell me. Go ahead and talk to it all you want, just don't ever say anything about it to me ever again."

Laurie's eyes widened. Her glasses made them look huge. "But there's more of them. Other faeries. They were running from something."

"I don't care," he said, wishing she would leave him alone. "I'm not allowed to play video games or watch TV for a week because of her and you."

"It's just a week," said Laurie. "Anyway, aren't you excited? We saw a real, live faerie. Just like Simon, Jared, and Mallory. A real faerie that needed our help."

Nicholas glared at her. How could she be so

stupid not to be afraid of that thing? It was horrible. It was alien. "Get out of my room. You already made me mess up my boat. You're not my sister, so stop acting like I care about what you have to say."

The color seemed to drain from Laurie's face.

Julian looked up from the bed once she left. His earbuds were still in, but Nick wondered how much he'd heard.

That night, Charlene got Chinese food for dinner. Nick picked at his lo mein until his dad finally told him to eat already. As Nick started shoveling down the noodles, Laurie cleared her throat.

"Um, mom?" she said, tucking her hair behind her ears.

Charlene stopped dipping her egg roll in hot mustard to look at her daughter.

"Mom, Nick promised me that he would go out to the big lake with me. We were going to sail one of his boats."

"I never said—" Nick sputtered. He hadn't promised anything like that.

"I thought you kept those things mint," Julian said, using one of his chopsticks to skewer a dumpling. He grinned. "What if the paint gets scratched?"

Nick glared at him and then turned his glare on Laurie for good measure.

She acted like she didn't notice, smiling like the suck-up she was. "I know that Nick's in trouble, but he can still go, right?"

Charlene looked over at Nick's dad expectantly. "Sure," he said slowly. "Fresh air. Better than sitting inside moping. Just make sure that you two get back before dark this time."

"But Dad—," Nick started.

"I don't want to hear it," Nick's dad said. "You're the one who made the promise."

Nick put down his fork, completely outmaneuvered. He couldn't believe it! She'd lied. Underneath that bizarro sparkly exterior, she was a devious, conniving liar.

He actually found himself grudgingly impressed.

When Nick stepped out onto the lawn the following morning, he did so with a sense of dread. "Why are you always making me come with you? Don't you have friends of your own?" He vaguely recalled girls shrieking with laughter in Charlene's backyard, when he and Jules had been forced to go there for dinner after the engagement. The house had been small, cluttered with handmade crafts and suncatchers. He'd felt like he was suffocating.

"Don't *you*?" Laurie snapped.

He stepped past Jules's spray-painted green car with two surfboards bungee-corded to a homemade roof rack. His dad's car sat in the driveway beside it, freshly waxed and gleaming. "I have lots of friends," he said, hoping she'd leave it alone.

Nick didn't like to think about the kids in the development he'd lived in before this one and how they were probably having tons of fun this summer. He used to clown around with them, just doing whatever. But that was a long time ago. Before his mom got sick. Before they moved. Before he started not bothering anyone.

Laurie sucked in her breath. "See her?" She held out her locket.

Nick snatched it, and the Sight sharpened his vision abruptly, making him dizzy. Where there had been only ripples before, he could clearly see a nixie frolicking in the lake. The melody that he'd thought was wind blowing through leaves and frogs croaking and birds singing changed in his ears to her song. It filled him with a swelling sense of longing for something that he couldn't quite describe. Still singing, she swam toward where he stood.

"Oh, crap," he said. He couldn't understand the words, but the melody shivered up his spine.

Laurie shifted the knapsack off her shoulder and took out two sandwiches and a bottle of soda.

"What's that for?" Nick asked. "You planning a picnic?"

Laurie shrugged, her freckled cheeks abruptly mottled with red. "I thought Taloa might like them."

"I looked in that book of yours," he said. "Don't they eat scum off the bottom of the lake or something?"

"Maybe she's never *had* a sandwich," said Laurie defensively. "It's just got celery in it."

"*Ooo-la-le-la, Nicholas.*" Taloa turned her froggy head to the side, clear membranes

53

blinking across her amphibious eyes. It seemed like she sang the words instead of speaking them. *"The heroic Nicholas. Ooo-le-la Laurie has told me the tale, of how you found my withered body. La-le-la and how the great Nicholas risked punishment from his elders for my sake."*

"Uh . . . um." Nick was unable to stop staring at the golden flecks in her unnervingly alien eyes.

"La-le-la the people I met before called me Taloa. You may call me that too-le-loo."

"Okay," he said, wondering what other

people she could have met, wondering too if she'd noticed that his palms were sweaty.

She smiled at him, revealing small, peglike teeth. *"I will shower you with my thanks. La-lum-le I will give you that which I gave your sister."* With that, Taloa grabbed his neck in her webbed hands and pulled him backward into the water.

He gulped water, choking, his eyes wide and looking up through the murk. His lungs hurt and he thrashed, Taloa's face floating above him, her fingers tight at his throat.

Then she let him go.

He sat up. Sputtering and coughing, he wiped his stinging eyes. "What the — ?"

The nixie laughed.

Laurie had a lopsided grin on her face. For a moment, she and Taloa both seemed completely alien and terrifying. He'd been drowning and

Laurie hadn't even tried to save him.

"You can give me back my locket now," Laurie said.

Nick just stared at her. "What?"

She walked over and reached to unclasp it. He pulled away, took the thing off himself, and dumped it in her hand. "Here."

"Look around," she said.

He was braced for the nixie to have disappeared, but she hadn't. He blinked a few times, but Taloa was still there. For a moment, panic flooded him.

"The water?" Nick asked. "It gave me the Sight?" The idea of *never* being able to *not* see faeries was horrible.

Laurie nodded. "Because she's been soaking in it."

Bushes rustled nearby. Nick spun toward the sound in time to see a creature the size of a large cat cradling a trash bag in its thin arms. It sat on its hind legs, three-toed claws digging into the dirt, and gazed at him with sand-colored eyes. Nick bit back a shout. "What's that? Do you see that?"

The nixie turned, but the creature was gone. Laurie looked where Nick pointed, squinting.

"It's gone," he said. "But I saw something."

The nixie swam closer. *"A hob-le-la. The forest fey fled during the burning. I only wish I le-lee knew where my sisters hopped le-la. Mayhaps you-le-loo could help."*

"There were more nixies in your pond?" Laurie asked, walking up to her. The edge of Laurie's ankle-length skirt trailed in the water.

"We were seven la-le," sang Taloa, her voice pitched high. *"Now I am only one."* She trailed off, looking at the woods miserably. *"The leaves do not*

It gazed at him with sand-colored eyes.

turn on their bellies le-lee. Le-la that means no more rain. I cannot look for them when the land is dry le-li. Please. La-la-look for me."

She looked so sad that, for a moment, it made her seem almost human. Almost.

"No way," Nick said.

"She gave you the Sight!" Laurie said.

He wanted to throttle her. "She tried to drown me!"

"She didn't mean to scare you," Laurie said consolingly. "She wouldn't have hurt you. It freaked me out too at first, but she was just playing."

Taloa bowed her head and sang, *"I would be grateful le-lo. The wetlands of our pond stretch le-la-le-lo-le-li in many directions. My sisters would follow the water. We may only live in our own water lo-le."*

Nick thought of how his father had made this pond by excavating mounds of dirt until the pit began to fill. All the wetlands in this area were probably connected. It would be too far for Taloa to hop, but he couldn't forget the feeling of her fingers at his neck. She'd wanted to scare him. She thought it was funny.

"I don't think so," Nick said.

Taloa's golden, froglike eyes narrowed. *"You will be sorry lo-le if you do not help la-lee me."*

"See?" Nick said. "Real nice."

"She doesn't mean it. She's just worried about her sisters."

"She's not a pet!" Nick said. "She's dangerous, and if you actually read that book you keep carrying around, you'd know it!" With that, he turned and stormed back to the house.

Laurie put the sandwiches and the cola on the bank and hurried after him. She looked back at Taloa several times as they walked back to the house, but Nick didn't slow down.

They turned up the driveway, and he noticed two things. One was that there were tons of little three-toed tracks in the dirt. The other was that his father's shiny new car was filled with sand.

They set out early the next morning.

Chapter Five

IN WHICH Nick Steps
onto More Trouble

It took them hours to sweep the last of the sand from his father's leather upholstery. Even after they'd pushed out the mounds onto the driveway and swept the seats with a broom and vacuumed the glove compartment with a car vacuum, they could still feel the gritty texture of it everywhere they touched.

"My dad's going to kill us," Nick said. He pushed back his sweaty hair.

Laurie groaned. "You should have just agreed to help her."

"Maybe," Nick said. "Fine. We'll go and look for her sisters." He turned toward the water. "FINE! WE'RE GOING, OKAY!" Then he looked at Laurie. "After we do this, we don't talk to it anymore, right? You swear?"

"She can't help it. She's —"

Nick cut her off. "Trouble! She's trouble!"

"You could have just told your dad that you didn't put the sand in his car," Laurie said.

"Sure. I could have pointed out all the little footprints, and he would have been completely convinced, right?"

Laurie ignored his sarcasm. "My mother believes me when I tell her things."

"No she doesn't," Nick said viciously. "She thinks it's cute you believe in faeries. That's all."

Laurie bit her lip thoughtfully.

"Swear you won't go talk to that thing anymore after we go on its quest."

"No," Laurie said finally. "You can't make me swear that."

"Fine." Nick made a final swipe with the broom and started toward the garage. "I can't make you do anything. Not like your nixie friend."

They walked into the kitchen. Nick put his head under the tap and turned it on. Laurie collapsed in a chair.

It was too late, and they were too tired, to go looking for Taloa's sisters. Nick and Laurie sat on the couches in the living room. When Nick's dad came home from supervising the construction, he looked over at them with a severe expression.

"The foreman saw you two messing around inside my car and it is absolutely *coated* with sand. What were you two doing?"

"We were cleaning it—"

"What's wrong with you lately, Nicholas? You used to be such a good kid. Did someone put you up to this?" Nick's dad looked over at Laurie.

"What are you implying, exactly?" Charlene asked. "Are you saying my daughter's responsible?"

"No!" Nick's dad said too quickly.

Charlene put her hand on her hip. "Of course not. That's the problem with your whole family. No one ever says what they really mean. Well, I'm not like that and Laurie's not like that, either."

She turned her back on him and walked out of the room before he could answer.

Nick went to bed feeling gleeful and guilty at the same time. He was so worn out that he fell asleep almost immediately, and if he had any dreams that night, he didn't remember them.

He and Laurie set out early the next morning, when the air was still cool and misty. Laurie didn't have a bike of her own, so she balanced herself on the handlebars of Nick's. He straddled the seat nervously. The bike had been a gift from his dad last Christmas, and he hadn't ridden it more than twice.

"Taloa said her old pond was past some big mangrove," Laurie said. "Do you know where that is?"

"Yeah. You can reach it from the trail," said Nick, starting to pedal. His mom had taken him and Jules out to the preserve when they were little and their father was at work. One time, they followed an armadillo, sneaking just enough behind it that it didn't notice, smothering their laughter. On another trip, they sat in the car with one of the windows rolled down a crack, calling in Spanish to get the attention of an alligator half-submerged in mud.

She'd picked out the location for the development and its name, Mangrove Hollow. *Cuenca de los Manglares*. But Nick's dad never talked about that anymore. Sometimes Nick was afraid he'd forget.

They sped down the trail, past a vibrant grasshopper that barely moved out of their way, past the place where the alligator had been sighted. And then, out of the corner of his eye, Nick saw a cloud of large insects. One darted out in front of him, and he could have sworn he saw a humanlike face on its chitinous body. He swatted the air in front of him, causing the bike to wobble.

"Watch it," said Laurie.

"Did you see that?" He glanced back, but it only looked like a rippling in the air, the

One darted out in front of him.

way gnats sometimes seem before you're close enough.

"What?" Laurie asked him, twisting around. They'd sped on far enough that he didn't think she'd see anything at all.

Nick turned back and stopped his dirt bike abruptly enough to make Laurie lose her balance on the handlebars. She yelped, but he was too busy staring openmouthed at the fire-blasted trees to notice what had happened to her.

"This is weird." He hopped off and absentmindedly leaned his bike against a tree.

"What's weird?" she asked with a glare.

Controlled burns were used in all the parks. He'd witnessed that plenty of times—smelled the scorched wood and seen the blackened trunks—even from the road. Nick's dad had explained how the burns kept the kind of wildfires that destroy houses from starting.

But something about this was different.

"It doesn't look right," he said.

"What do you mean?" Laurie asked.

He shook his head, not sure himself.

Where there had once been a shallow wetlands pond, there was only cracked dirt. On the outer edge of the burnt area, leaves hung like shriveled rags from charcoal limbs. Smoldered ferns drooped over seared moss. Everything was still. No cicadas buzzed, no birds called.

The more he looked at the burnt area, the more he thought that it didn't seem controlled at all. No trees could grow back from this, at least not for a long time. And it stretched out in two directions, starting near where the water had been, like two great blasts had been shot at random from a flamethrower.

He walked up a sandy hill to get a better view. The earth seemed soft under his feet, and he wondered if that was another piece of evidence.

"Hey," he said. "Come feel this."

Laurie didn't answer. He turned to see her watching three ashen shapes like she was waiting for them to move. They looked oddly like bent black branches, or maybe bodies.

He swallowed hard and then took a deep breath. His voice shook anyway. "I guess we should tell Taloa that we didn't find her friends."

"*Sisters,*" said Laurie, a hitch in her voice. Her eyes were wet. "They were her sisters."

"Sisters." Nick echoed. The word felt strange in his mouth. He jumped off the hill, and as he did, the hill rose.

Black eyes blinked slowly in the sandy soil. A massive swell curled into a fist. Roots ripped loose where vast limbs had been half-buried. The ground split and an enormous creature rose from it. Laurie screamed. The sound snapped Nick out of stunned staring and into action.

He ran toward his bike. As he threw one leg over the frame, he looked back.

The hill was standing, towering over them. It was wider than their house. Taller than the cranes that towered over the construction site.

"Get on!" he yelled. Laurie stumbled, her long skirt catching in the spokes as she hopped up on the seat. Nick pedaled anyway, hearing the

He pedaled hard.

fabric rip and feeling her fingers dig into his back.

"It'sfollowingit'sfollowingit'sfollowing," Laurie said, her voice high and urgent.

Branches snapped, something thudded, and the ground shook. The bike wobbled and turned on its side. They both fell. Nick's knees burned and his head was ringing as he pulled himself back on his feet. Laurie was already up, her skirt torn and her cheek smeared with dirt. Blood stained her lip, and the chain around her neck had snapped.

The giant loomed above them, bellowing. Sand and dirt rained from its maw.

Nick lifted the bike as one of the giant's feet slammed down beside him. Something wasn't quite right with the front tire, but he didn't have time to do anything but hope as he hopped onto it. Laurie got on behind him. He pedaled hard, wishing that he'd ridden his bike more, that he was more athletic, that his legs would move faster. If Julian had been there, he would have biked so fast the giant would never have caught them, but Nick was slow and they were going to be crushed because of it.

Nick ignored his ragged breathing, ignored the pain in his muscles, ignored the sounds of smashing and crashing behind them and the dust pluming around them. Sweat rolled down his forehead and stung his eyes. He concentrated on pumping his legs.

"Right behind us," Laurie squeaked.

Nick jerked the handlebars hard to the left, like he'd seen people in car chases on TV do, but instead of veering onto another path, he hit an embankment. The bike jumped into the air. He gritted his teeth and tried to hold it steady. This time they didn't tip when they hit dirt. Nick just kept pedaling, faster and faster, as they sped through the woods.

"How about now?" he asked, grinning. He couldn't believe how good that had felt. He wanted to cheer.

"He's looking for us," Laurie whispered. "Stop the bike! We have to hide."

Nick hit the brakes. Laurie's head banged into the back of his.

"Ow!" she said.

"Shhhh." They stumbled off the bike, dropping it onto the grass. One wheel still spun. Nick got down on his hands and knees, crawling toward a large palmetto bush.

They were close enough to the development that they could probably make it on foot from this point. He looked back, trying to see the giant through the dense foliage. It seemed like the giant was rooting around in the dirt. Then, lifting a miniscule wriggling thing in between two massive fingers, it dropped the thing into its mouth.

"What's it doing?" Nick whispered. "Eating a lizard?"

Laurie had taken off her glasses. It was only then that he noticed the bridge had cracked and her glasses were now in two separate pieces. "It's not supposed to be like this," she said numbly.

"Like what?"

The massive creature opened its mouth and breathed hard, like it expected something to happen. It breathed again.

"Laurie! Concentrate. What's it doing?"

She squinted. "In the Guide, giants—that's got to be a giant—um, I think they eat lizards." She stopped. "Oh."

"What?"

"They eat *salamanders* to breath fire." Laurie

It dropped the thing into its mouth.

lifted one dirty finger to push back her glasses automatically, but there were no more glasses, so she just smeared the ridge of her nose with grime.

Nick felt suddenly light-headed, as though all the insanity hit him at once and it was too much for his brain to comprehend. "Why would salamanders make it breathe fire? And if they do, why isn't it working?"

"Not all salamanders are faeries. The Guide thinks the magic ones might be baby dragons or something. I guess the giant can't tell the difference."

"We better get out of here before he finds the right one. Just stay low to the ground. We'll have to crawl."

Laurie put her hand on his arm. "Wait. Look."

The giant had stopped. With a sigh, he turned

Overleaf
Laurie's flyer for the
book signing at Robot Books

and started to pick his way back through the trees. Nick let out a breath he didn't even know he was holding. Laurie sagged to the ground.

In the distance, Nick heard the faint sound of music. In a man-made lake in Mangrove Hollow, the nixie was singing her creepy, melodic song.

The giant swung around, cocking his head. Then, lurching forward and knocking aside trees, he crashed toward the development.

Listening as if transfixed

Chapter Six

IN WHICH Laurie Reconsiders Things

Nicholas and Laurie didn't speak as they ran home, saving every bit of energy for going faster. In all that time, Nick had pictured so many horrible possibilities that he was stunned to find the giant sitting beside the lake, picking at the dirt and listening to the nixie's song as if transfixed. Its features were relaxed, its black eyes fixed on Taloa with calm adoration.

"He's not doing anything," Nick whispered.

Laurie smoothed back her ragged hair. Her

skirt was so torn that part of it followed her on the ground like the train on a wedding dress. "Maybe if you don't step on him again he won't go crazy."

"He looked like a hill!" Nick said. "If it wasn't for me—" He broke off as Taloa scrambled onto the bank. The giant's large eyes followed her every move.

"*La-lo-le,*" she sang, between notes of the other tune. She bared her teeth. *"You led him here, lo-le."*

"He heard you singing!" said Nick. "This is your fault, not mine!"

She brought her face close enough that he could smell the pond mud on her skin. The long, drooping weeds of her hair stuck to her neck. *"Lo-le, where are my sisters, Nicholas?"*

The giant swung its massive head in their direction, grunting. The ground shook as it rose.

"Sing, Taloa!" Laurie said. "I don't think it likes it when you stop singing!"

"We grew tired," said Taloa, and although she sang the words, they didn't seem to calm the giant. It wasn't the right tune. The massive nostrils flared. *"Our throats were hoarse lo-le-lo. That's when he began lo-le to blow fire."*

"Taloa, please," Nick said. "Please sing."

"Where are my sisters, Nicho-le-lo-las?"

"Burned," he said, not meaning for it to sound so blunt and sad. He didn't know how to cushion it better, didn't have time to think with the giant looming over them.

Taloa shuffled back, crouching, the webbing of her fingers pulled tight between spread fingers. A low sound came from the back of her throat.

"Only three of them," Laurie said. "We don't know where the others are. They might be fine!"

"She's right. There were only three bodies. You have to sing! We saved you, remember? We even looked for your sisters . . ." Nick tried to keep his voice level but couldn't. The shadow of the giant fell over them as it stepped one foot into the pond. Waves splashed along the shore.

"I repaid my lo-le-la debt when I gave la-le-la you

the Sight. But le-lo, I will sing if you will repay lo-le me by finding all my le-la sisters."

"Of course we will," Nick said, looking at the giant. "We will. We promise!"

She did sing, then, the haunting music spilling out of her throat, her head thrown back. The giant settled down again, trailing its fingers in the water. It blinked sleepily, burrowing down a little in the mud.

Nick let out all his breath in a rush.

"I have an idea," said Laurie, pulling on Nick's sleeve. "Back at the house."

"Be lo-lee-le swift. I don't know how long I can keep singing. My voice will tire."

"Just try, Taloa," Nick said, looking into her golden eyes for any sign that she would. But all he saw was his own face reflected in the liquid depths.

Laurie led him to the house, through the

garage, inside and up the stairs. Nick expected Laurie to pick up one of the books off her shelves, but she went to the computer instead.

"The signing I was telling you about. With the people who made the field guide." She clicked through the pages until she found what she was looking for. "See? Tomorrow night they have a signing at Robot Books. We can ask them what to do."

He looked at her incredulously. "We're going to just leave that thing out there? For a whole day? What if Taloa can't keep singing?"

"Well, the Spiderwick people are on tour, right? Maybe there's another event tonight." She scrolled up. "Orlando. It's not *that* far. Do you think your dad would drive us?"

Nick shook his head. There was no way. "What about your mom?"

Laurie shook her head. "She'd tell me that

I have to be
patient, since I
already told her
about the Robot's
signing a million
times. Also, she'll
be mad I broke my
glasses."

"Give them to me,"
Nick said.

She handed over the pieces,
and Nick took them to Jules's room.
Laurie followed him. He grabbed a tube of
glue and carefully squeezed a dollop onto the
broken plastic. Then he put the two pieces into
jeweler's clamps and pressed them together.
"It should hold for a while. It's probably better
than tape."

"Thanks," she said, although she didn't sound

that thankful. The tone of her voice was odd. Then he placed it: She sounded defeated.

Nick bit the inside of his lip, considering. "Maybe you should tell your mom the truth. If you think she'd believe you. We still have the clover, right?"

Her neck was bare.

Laurie scrabbled at her chest for the locket, but it was gone. "I lost it! I lost the picture of my father and I don't have another one."

Nick didn't understand the big deal. Her father wasn't dead; couldn't she just get another photo? But all he knew about Laurie's father was that he had a motorcycle.

Laurie shook her head. "You were right before. Mom would just tell me that I had a good imagination. She'd think it was cute."

Nick couldn't even imagine what his own father would say.

Laurie took an unsteady breath. "I didn't think it would be like this. I mean, I read the field guide. I knew there were monsters. I just didn't think we'd find any. I thought we'd see sprites or something pretty." She paused. "I guess I didn't think we'd see anything at all."

"But you said that all that stuff was real."

"I wanted it to be real," she said. "I thought

that if I acted like it was true, then it would be almost like it was. Just like I thought it would be so cool to have a brother and we're almost the exact same age, so I thought it was going to be great. I hate it. I hate you, and I really hate faeries." Walking over to her bed, she flopped down on it, hiding her head in her arms.

Nick wanted not to care. He told himself that he already had a family. He didn't need an annoying sister. He didn't even want a sister. He couldn't remember ever wanting a sister. He opened his mouth to tell her so, when he remembered what he did have. An annoying brother.

"Jules," he said. "Maybe Jules would drive us."

Jules was on his phone.

Jules was on his cell phone when they found him, talking to his girlfriend as he killed zombies on the downstairs TV screen.

"I could ride any wave on this beach," he said. "I don't care what Doug said. You know what a dirtbag he is."

"Jules," Nick said.

Jules looked over at them and made swatting motions toward the door.

"Jules!" Nick yelled.

"Hold on," Jules said into the phone. "My little brother has a bug up his butt." Then he laughed. Finally, he held the phone away from his ear. On the television, a zombie dressed like a fireman was eating his character's head.

"We need you to drive us to Orlando. To a book signing."

"Um, lemme think," Jules said, tapping the

phone to his chin. "Negatory. Never. No way. Get out of here."

There was no point to even trying to explain the truth to Jules. It would take way too long and seem way too easy to dismiss as some pretend game. "What if I said I had a video of you lifting weights and talking to yourself in the mirror?" Nick made his voice deep. "'Looking good. Yeah. How do you like that, ladies?'"

JULIAN VARGAS

"Shut up, dillweed." Jules got up, clicking

his phone closed and jumping over the couch in a single motion.

"You just hung up on . . . ," Laurie started.

Nick backed into the wall, raising his hands in surrender. "Look, I'll delete it off the camera. As soon as we get back from Orlando."

Jules towered over him. The cell started to buzz. "You're talking about an hour-plus drive each way. How about you just delete it now and never mention it again?"

"*Please,*" Laurie said, making her eyes huge and putting one hand on his arm. "It's just that they're my *favorite* authors and they were going to come here, but now they're not. This is the only way I'll get to see them and I've been waiting *forever.*" She paused. "And Nick really likes them too."

"Why can't your mom take you? Or Dad?"

"They're busy," Laurie said. "They were

going to take me—us—to the signing here, but it got canceled."

Nick's mouth opened and closed. He was stunned by the audacity of her lie.

Jules blinked at her, like he had no idea what to do. "Okay, okay," he said finally, deflated. "Why didn't you say so in the first place?" He flipped open his phone. "I'll ask Cindy if she wants to come."

Nick looked at Laurie in astonishment. He had no idea where she'd learned it, but she sure knew how to get people to do what she wanted.

Jules dropped them off.

Chapter Seven

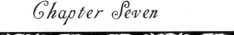

IN WHICH We Nearly
Break the Fourth Wall

The giant squatted beside the lake and turned black eyes toward them as they hopped in Jules's car. The hot seat burned the small strip of Nick's thighs not covered by his shorts. He kicked aside fast-food wrappers and shoved a damp beach towel under his legs.

"Okay," Laurie said. "I printed out directions. It should take us approximately an hour and fifteen minutes if there's no traffic. Also, I printed alternative directions in case we need them."

"Uh, okay." Jules took the directions from her. "You ready, Nick?"

"Sure," Nick said, never taking his eyes off the giant.

Beside him, Laurie fidgeted with her books and did the same.

A few minutes later, they pulled into Cindy's driveway. She hopped into the front seat, puka shells swinging from her braids.

"Hey," she said, sitting backward so she could look at them. "How are you guys?"

"Okay," said Laurie.

"Fine," Nick said, tight lipped. What he really wanted to do was yell, *There's a giant on our lawn and we're all going to die. How do you think we are?*

Cindy leaned over and gave him a squeeze on the shoulder that made him smile despite himself.

She and Jules spent the whole drive talking

about the different beaches near the bookstore and different surf shops and whether they might have the kind of wax that Cindy liked. Out the window, Nick watched as they sped by roadkill being chewed on by a cougarlike creature that had a barbed tail. He gasped, and Cindy looked back at him. He just shook his head. For a moment, he wanted to tell her everything, but then she turned to the front seat and his brother said something, and it was too late.

CINDY

By the time Jules dropped them off at the bookstore, Nick was vibrating with anxiety. The event had already started.

"Here's my cell," Jules said, handing over the phone. "We're going to check out the surf shops—buzz us on Cindy's line when you're done."

"Okay," Nick said. Laurie was already inside the bookstore doors.

"Don't talk to strangers!" Cindy called as the car started to roll away.

The icy air-conditioning and the scent of coffee washed over Nick as he entered. He walked to the edge of the crowd, watching a plump woman dressed entirely in black and a spiky-haired man in a bright blazer. The man had a pad of paper set up on an easel and was drawing a dragon.

"Is that them?" Nick whispered to Laurie.

She nodded, not even looking at him. Her fingers gripped the edge of her books tightly. "What if they don't believe these are from home?"

"What?"

"The books. What if someone thinks I stole them?"

"Calm down," said Nick.

"I don't even have a receipt! What if they take my books? I don't have any way to prove that they're mine. Maybe I should write my name in them. But what if they see me writing?"

"Shut up!" Nick said, and Laurie bit her lip, like her teeth were actually forcing her mouth closed.

After the man demonstrated various hand-raising techniques, he offered the drawing to anyone who could answer a trivia question. Nick raised his hand.

HOLLY BLACK

"You haven't read the books!" hissed Laurie, her arm waving frantically.

It didn't matter, since the woman picked a girl near the front. The girl answered correctly some question about a pig squealing.

Then, finally, they were taking questions from the audience. Nick's hand shot up so fast that the woman pointed to him.

"What's your question?" she asked. Her eyes were outlined in black, like a cartoon character's.

"I have a problem with a giant," said Nick.

Some of the audience, including a few parents, laughed.

"I am not some stupid kid," he said, his face going hot with embarrassment and anger. "I'm being serious. It got one of those salamander things and it burned up a pond full of nixies. It followed the singing of the

only one that escaped to my dad's development and the singing is keeping it happy for right now, but I don't know what it's going to do next. How can I stop it?"

The plump woman looked over at the guy. He raised his eyebrows like he was glad he wasn't the one fielding that question.

"Well," she said, "wearing red might help protect you . . . and, um, iron."

"But how do I get rid of it?"

She frowned. "You might want to look at fairy tales—'Jack the Giant Killer,' 'The Giant and the Tailor,' 'The Young Giant.' Those are all about someone small outwitting someone large. I don't have any more specific suggestion than that, but since you're the hero of your own story, I know you'll come up with a good ending." She smiled, but Nick was pretty sure she was smiling more at her own ability to make up something that sounded like an answer than at him.

"We have to take another question," the guy said. "Good luck with that giant."

The audience laughed again. Nick's face went hot. Beside him, Laurie looked stricken.

"They didn't believe you," she said.

"Come on," Nick said. He steered her over to the store's café and sat down backward in one of the chairs. "Whatever with them. They're nothing but fakes."

Laurie clutched her field guide to her chest. She looked like she was going to cry.

Nick thumbed open his brother's cell. "I'll call Jules. We've got to get back. We just wasted a lot of time." For a moment, he thought about calling home—checking to make sure the house was still there, that they weren't already too late.

Laurie wasn't listening to him, anyway. She was staring at a black-haired boy about their age. The boy waved to someone standing off the stage—a woman with red hair standing near a table covered with props supposedly from Arthur Spiderwick.

"Do you know that kid?" Nick asked.

Laurie stood up. "He looks familiar," she said.

The boy walked back into the aisles of books, and Laurie followed him. Nick followed Laurie, tucking Jules's cell back in his pocket.

"I know you're upset about the Spiderwick people not turning out like you hoped, but I don't think stalking some —"

"Shhhh," she said.

The boy had walked up to another black-haired kid standing in front of the natural history section. For a moment, Nick blinked in confusion. They were mirror images of each other. Then he realized: twins.

"Jared and Simon Grace," Laurie whispered. "They look just like their pictures."

They were mirror images of each other.

Nick was puzzled. "What pictures?"

"It says in all the Spiderwick books that the information came from real kids. Jared, Simon, and Mallory Grace."

"I don't know—," Nick started, but Laurie was already heading toward the boys. There was nothing to do but follow her.

"Excuse me," she said. "Are you Jared?"

They laughed. One of the boys shifted a stack of bird guides to his other arm. "Who wants to know?"

"*Laurie,*" Nick cautioned.

"What are you doing here?" Laurie asked, clearly taking the boy's question as confirmation she was right. "Are you part of the book tour?"

"Nah. Our dad's shooting a TV pilot," Jared said. "Wanted us to come stay with him for the summer. I think he figured we'd spend the whole time riding roller coasters. Anyway, we thought we'd come to the signing. See what one was like."

"I think Arthur would have liked it," Simon said. "Pretty convincing."

"So you admit it!" Laurie said. "You really are them!"

"Did you hear our question?" Nick asked.

"Sure," Jared said. "A giant, right? That was pretty funny."

"The giant's real," said Laurie said. "We have the Sight. I've read the whole field guide a dozen times at least."

"Too bad there's nothing really useful in it," Nick said.

"Nick!" Laurie's eyes went wide with horror.

"You're serious about the giant?" Simon said.

"Stick-a-needle-in-my-eye serious," said Nick.

"Faeries can be pretty big on putting out the eyes of people who can see them," said Jared.

Nick put his hand automatically to his face.

"We really need your help," Laurie said.

"Prove it," Jared said. "Prove that you really saw something."

Laurie looked at Nick. He wanted to wipe the smug expression off Jared's face. "How?"

Jared shrugged. "Not my problem."

Nick thought about all the weird stuff in the field guide—the way that brownies could turn into boggarts if you made them mad enough or how tiny stone mice were evidence of a basilisk in the area. But remembering any of those bits of trivia only proved that Nick had read parts of their book.

He thought about Taloa and the giant and the weird thing with the sand-colored eyes and the bug with the human face. "I don't know," Nick said. "I just wish that I could go back to thinking this was all stupid, made-up crap."

"Not my problem."

"That's pretty convincing, actually," said Simon.

"Okay, let's say we believe you. I don't know much about giants," Jared said. "I'll call home and see what Mallory can find in Uncle Arthur's notes. It's going to take her a while to look through everything."

"You want to meet us here tomorrow?" asked Simon.

Laurie shook her head. "We don't live that close."

Jared took Laurie's field guide out of her hands and wrote down his phone number on the back inside flap. "Call and we'll tell you what we find out."

Laurie took back the book with shaking hands. Nick turned his head so no one could see him rolling his eyes. He didn't care if there were a million books about Jared and Simon.

Books didn't always tell the whole story. As he walked out the door of the store, punching Cindy's number into the cell phone, he couldn't help worrying that they'd wasted time.

He didn't think they had a lot of time left.

The giant roared, beating its chest.

Chapter Eight

IN WHICH a Plan Is Hatched

Nicholas kept waking up that night. The haunting, desperate nixie song hummed in his ears and woke him out of his dreams.

He thought of the giant, with his dirt-encrusted skin, his thatched hair, and the moss and plants that grew across his shoulders. He thought of the gaze from those small black eyes catching on lamps inside the house. Would the giant think the lights were pretty? Worth investigating? Worth pulling apart a house to get to?

For a giant, coming across Mangrove Hollow

must be like coming across a sandcastle on a beach. He might ignore it as long as he's busy with other fun things, but if he gets bored, he's going to either play with it or kick it over.

Please keep singing, Nick thought. *Keep singing.*

When he woke again, it was still dark outside. Dark and quiet. For a moment, he couldn't think why he was awake.

Standing, he walked to the window and looked out. His hands felt clammy. He rubbed them against the cloth of his pajama pants.

Then he remembered. He couldn't hear any singing. For a moment, he felt sick. Then he opened the door of the bedroom and took the stairs two at a time.

A horrible cracking noise and a bright flare of light at the windows made him go faster.

Outside, flames made it easy to see. One of the trees was on fire, leaves blazing. The giant roared, beating its chest. Nick ran across the wet grass, sliding in the mud to where Taloa was crawling to her feet.

She stared upward in horror, clearly dazed. *"I fell asleep la-lo."* Her voice cracked.

"Sing!" he shouted. "Get up! Sing!"

The giant looked down at them, inhaling deeply.

Taloa opened her mouth and the sound that came out was closer to a croak than any melody.

"Sing!" Nick screamed.

Somehow, her voice shaking, she managed a few notes of the tune. *"La-lo-le-le-la-lo-le-le."*

The giant slumped beneath a scrub oak with a loud thud, watching Taloa with greedy eyes. Somehow he must have found a salamander. Nick only hoped he hadn't found a nest of them.

"Lo-le-lee. Nicholas. My sisters. Remember. Lo-le-la-le-la."

Nick nodded.

Taking a deep breath, Taloa sang more steadily, her voice growing more confident with each note. Nick sank to his knees as the sky began to lighten in the east.

"There's a big mound of dirt over by the lake," Nick's father said, waving his coffee cup in that direction. "Over by the lightning strike. What idiot dumped it there?"

Outside, the sky was dark and heavy with rain. Nick's stomach was sour with tension and lack of sleep.

Laurie jumped up. "The mound looks nice," she said. "Like landscaping. You shouldn't try and move it."

Charlene squinted at her daughter. The

cup in her hand had been one of Nick's mom's favorites. Nick wished she would put it down. "Honey, I think it looks like a big pile of dirt."

"No!" Laurie's voice came out high. "Don't go near it."

"Maybe you should listen to her," Nick said. He had the portable phone clutched in one hand.

As soon as his dad and Charlene walked out the door, he was going to call Jared. Bowls of cereal long gone soggy sat on the table. Neither he nor Laurie could bring themselves to eat.

"I'll get someone to remove it first thing tomorrow," his father said.

Nick opened his mouth to say something. He wanted to tell his father about the giant. He wanted, more than anything, for his dad to listen to *him* and not to Laurie and Charlene.

Charlene grabbed her purse off the counter. "Bye, kids."

"Keep out of trouble," said Nick's father. Then he was gone.

Laurie grabbed for the phone and dialed. Reaching over, Nick hit the speaker button. The ringing crackled loudly in the room.

"Mallory found something," said Jared, without any greeting. "You are so lucky. Next week she's leaving for fencing camp, and my aunt Lucy can't see too well."

"Yeah," Nick said irritably. "We're real lucky. What did she find?"

"Turns out that my uncle Arthur corresponded with someone who lived not too far from you guys. A specialist on giants. There were a bunch of notes on different types and behaviors. I guess there were a lot back then or something. Anyway, I have an address."

Nick groaned. "How old is this address?"

There was a long silence on the other end of the line. "Pretty old."

"It's all we've got," Nick said. "Give it to me."

"Okay, it's on Swamp Road. Number eleven. I looked at a map—that's probably fifteen minutes from you. I'm leaving now. I'll meet you there."

"You're coming?" Laurie asked happily.

"There might be some letters and drawings of our uncle's. Dad left Simon and me some money for food and whatever, so I can use that to get a cab. We used to cab everywhere in New York."

"Is Simon coming with you?" she asked.

"He's got to stay here and answer the phone when Dad calls," said Jared. "He can do my voice pretty well if Dad asks to talk to me."

"See you soon," Laurie said sweetly, and Nick made a gagging sound. She fumbled to click the phone off so fast that she knocked it to the floor.

"I wish we had the bike," said Nick. Sweat soaked the back of his shirt, and he regretted

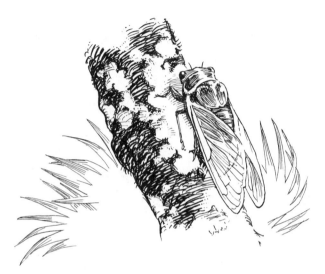

all the equipment he'd decided to lug with them. His school backpack thumped heavily against his back with each step. Cicadas droned ceaselessly in the trees.

They'd followed the streets on another printout of Laurie's until the sidewalks ran out and the asphalt went pitted and cracked as the road turned to dirt.

They passed a house with a dog that started barking, pawing at a chain-link fence. Nick almost expected the owners to come out, but the windows of the house were dark and empty. There was a car parked in the driveway, but judging from the state of its rusty body and blown-out tires, no one had driven it in a while. Thunderclouds roiled overhead.

Nick shivered, despite the heat. "It's weird that there's nobody around. It's like no one lives here."

"Stop trying to freak me out," said Laurie.

"What?" Nick demanded. "I wasn't."

"I had no idea that having a brother would be so *irritating*."

"Look," he said. "I didn't ask for our parents to get married. There's no point in being mad at me. Maybe they'll split up."

She narrowed her eyes. "It's just that, before, Mom and I lived in our own house, by ourselves.

We talked about stuff. I could say what I was thinking and do what I wanted. It was my space and I could be me. I had room."

"Now you have *my* room."

She frowned at him. "You can have it back. The giant's going to burn it down anyway." She looked away and sighed. "Everything was better when I was imagining it. Real things are complicated."

"You're right," Nick said with a groan. "This is pointless. We're not heroes. Taloa's going to stop singing, and we're just trying to make ourselves feel better chasing down dumb leads."

Laurie pointed to a sign. "Swamp Road. Our dumb lead."

Swamp Road was framed on both sides with scrubby wetlands and dotted with a few dilapidated houses. The fourth had the correct number nailed to its sagging aluminum cladding,

It looked long abandoned.

although it looked long abandoned.

They walked across a lawn of sugar sand and patches of crabgrass to a tiny house with a rusted metal door. The roof was sunken in the middle, and the siding hung off in sheets. They heard a steady creaking, like an old door swinging in the wind. Rusted rakes, buckets, and old tarps littered a ramshackle porch.

"I don't think anyone's here," said Laurie. She walked up to the door and gave it a push. "It's open."

"Don't do that!" Nick grabbed her arm. "Some nice giant expert might have lived here a bazillion years ago, but any creep could live here now."

"Hello!" Laurie called, ignoring him.

There was no answer. Laurie banged her fist against the worn wood.

A light shone where the yard sloped into

dense bushes. Then the light jerked to one side.

"Jared," Nick yelled, walking toward it. "Is that you?"

Rain started to fall, hard, muffling the sound of his voice.

"Looked like a flashlight," Laurie said, pulling up her jacket to cover her head.

They followed the glow down to where the mud started sucking at the bottoms of their shoes.

"Hello," Laurie shouted. "Please. We just need some answers."

Then the light started moving fast, like the person holding it had started running.

"Follow it," Nick said. They took off across the wetlands. Laurie sprinted ahead, but even as fast as she was going, the light seemed to be moving faster.

Nick stopped, breathing hard. The rain obscured his sight. "Laurie!"

Something darted toward him and he shouted. It seemed like a jellyfish swimming through the air, its center incandescent. Two small stalks on its head might have been eyes, but the tiny wings at its back were far too small to keep it aloft.

The second light zoomed away from him.

"Laurie!" he shouted. "They're faeries! Jared's not out here! Come back!"

When he turned around, nothing was familiar. His tracks had already been absorbed by the soft, wet soil or turned to widening puddles by the rain, and he had no idea how to retrace his steps.

"Laurie?" he shouted. He couldn't see her in all the rain and dark. "Laurie!"

Several more lights zoomed close, whirling around him. Suddenly it seemed like the field

"They're faeries!"

was full of glowing jellyfish. They zipped past, turning him this way and that. He tried to grab one and fell in the mud.

Rain fell on his face like tears. There, as he looked up at the lights, a strange sense of serenity washed over him. They seemed like a shifting kaleidoscope of stars.

"Nick?" Laurie called. She sounded frightened. He shook himself.

"Laurie," he said. "I'm here! Come toward my voice."

"Will-o'-the-wisps," she called, collapsing beside him. "I remember them from the book. They could have led us off a cliff or into quicksand."

"Good thing there's practically no cliffs in Florida," he said, but the goose bumps rose on his skin.

Laurie's face was flushed, and mud streaked her

chest and arms. One of her flip-flops was gone.

"I fell," she said, by way of explanation.

"We've got to get out of here. I think the house is back that way," he said, but he couldn't see it.

She shook her head and pointed through the rain. "No, I think it's over there."

The lights darted in the distance, and Nick suddenly thought of how much worse it would have been to be lost like this at night, how they might have wandered for hours, deeper and deeper into the brush.

"It's this way!" Nick insisted, starting to walk. "It's got to be."

"Okay," she said, following. But she didn't look convinced; she looked scared. "Does this look familiar?"

He wasn't sure. They'd been running. "Yes," he said. "This has to be the way."

"I don't think it looks like the way."

"It's the way!" Nick yelled.

A distant voice called something that sounded like their names from behind them.

Nick frowned. "More faerie tricks?"

"Laurie! Nick!" the voice said.

"It's Jared." Laurie waved around her arms. "Jared! We're over here! Keep yelling."

They followed his voice back to the house, their feet sinking in the mud. Nick didn't admit he'd been wrong about the direction, and Laurie didn't call him on it.

Jared stood on the slope of the backyard in jeans and a T-shirt, waving to them. A messenger bag was slung over his shoulder. Nick and Laurie scrambled up the hill.

"What were you guys doing?" Jared asked with a knowing smirk.

"We thought we saw something," Nick said. Laurie looked like she was ready to

Jared stood on the slope.

open her mouth and tell him about the whole, embarrassing adventure, so he spoke as firmly as possible. *"But we didn't."*

Laurie pointed toward the house. "I don't think anyone's home."

"The door's open," said Jared. "Maybe we could take a quick look inside in case whoever used to live here isn't coming back."

"Okay," Nick said.

As they walked back to the front door, Nick thought about the odd, floating wisps and shivered. Maybe Arthur Spiderwick's correspondent had followed their lights, too. Maybe he had never found his way back.

Laurie stepped onto faded linoleum, trying to keep her bare feet off the dirty floor as much as possible. The first room was a kitchen. A teakettle sat beside a huge crab pot on the stove, and a refrigerator hummed in the opposite corner. The electricity was still on, Nick thought. Someone had to live here.

He followed Laurie down a narrow hallway, where only a calendar from 1971 hung. To his right, something moved, and he turned, heart thudding, to find himself looking into a cloudy mirror. Jared grinned at him in the reflection.

"Hey, come here," Laurie called.

Nick forced himself to follow, although his instincts screamed for him to get out. This wasn't the kind of house a sane person lived in.

Laurie stood in the middle of a rickety living room. An old chair with stuffing and springs popping out of it stood in front of a rabbit-eared television. Laurie pointed to a door that stood partially ajar.

Nick crossed the living room to where she was indicating. It was an oddly shaped

room, too small to be a
comfortable bedroom,
and it was covered in
paper. Drawings,
documents, and
pages of notes
covered a small
metal desk,
carpeted the
floor, and had
been tacked up or
glued all over the
walls. He stepped
closer. Illustrations of
giants. Dozens and dozens
of them. Some giants were
bound with ropes. Another had had its head
cut clean off. Articles about fires. Newspaper
clippings.

JARED GRACE

139

PARCHED BY DROUGHT, FLORIDA'S FIRES SPREAD, **read one.** LARGE SMOKE PLUME OVER ATLANTIC. LANDSLIDE CAUSE STILL UNEXPLAINED. FIRE SUPPRESSION INEFFECTIVE.

"Um, this is kind of weird." Nick held up an illustration of a giant with a rope connecting its ankle to its neck. "Pretty smart, though. It can't stand up."

Jared walked into the room. "Whoa."

Nick cocked his head to one side. The illustration reminded him of the diagrams that he used to put his models together. Tab A into slot B. Finally, something that made sense. "We could maybe climb a tree. Use some rope like a lasso. The ankle part would be easy."

"This has a really creepy, crazy-person vibe to it," Laurie said. "Who was this guy?"

Rifling through the papers, Jared pulled out a few illustrations.

"What's that?" asked Nick.

"My uncle Arthur did these, based on the notes he'd gotten. According to the letter Mallory found, he'd sent a bunch of art down for confirmation." Jared started to roll them up. "I would have never even seen them if we didn't come here. I have to show these to Simon!"

"Wait a minute," Nick said. "You can't just take those papers."

"Why not?" asked Jared, pointing to the diagram in Nick's hand. "Aren't you going to take that?"

"That's different! I *need* this. We have to stop that giant and we have to follow the instructions *precisely*. You're just stealing!"

"I'm not stealing," Jared said. "These were supposed to be sent back. Anyway, my great-great-uncle wrote to this guy more than eighty years ago. Didn't you see that ancient calendar? He's probably long gone."

"I don't think so," said Laurie softly. She ran her fingers over one of the newspaper articles on the wall. "This is from last year. And the electricity works."

Jared shrugged. "Whatever. You got what you wanted and I got what I wanted, so let's get out of here."

"You're not going to help us?" Laurie asked.

Jared shook his head. "What? First you call me a thief and then you want my help?"

"You're the faerie guy. You're supposed to be good at this stuff." Nick pointed a finger at him and narrowed his eyes. "Unless it was all hype."

"You better shut up, lard ass," Jared said.

"I bet none of that stuff in the books ever even happened to you. You probably made it up."

"Shut up!" Jared grabbed his collar, fist cocking back for a punch. Nick closed his eyes, throwing up his hands.

"Stop it!" Laurie shouted. "Stop fighting, you morons!"

Nick opened his eyes. Jared was breathing hard, fist still clenched.

Laurie laughed. "Oh my god, you are just

"You better shut up, lard ass."

like the books! You really are Jared Grace."

"Jared Fennelly*, actually," Jared said, letting out a long breath. "Mom made them change our last name."

*Still not his real name.

Its enormous eyes fixed on Taloa.

Chapter Nine

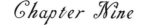

IN WHICH They Go According to the Plans, but the Plans Go Awry

Nick, Laurie, and Jared ran back to the development, the plans for subduing the giant rolled and tucked away in Nick's backpack.

The giant was still squatting beside the pond when they got there, its enormous eyes fixed on Taloa as rainwater ran off its rocky back. The water faerie's song sounded slower and more subdued, and her voice seemed rough. The nixie looked at them with desperation as they came to the edge of the water.

"Just a little longer," Laurie promised.

"I can sing a little longer lo-le-li," sang the nixie, *"for you that saved me."*

Jared stared at her and said nothing.

Wire cable would be strong enough to hold the giant once they'd lassoed him. It was easy to get rope from the construction site, but Nick worried it'd snap. They took what wire they could find and bound it together.

Rain fell in sheets, making the knotting slippery. Nick took a quick look back at the house. He didn't see his father's car, but that didn't mean much. He hoped his father and Jules and Charlene stayed far enough away that even if this didn't work, they'd be safe.

"Who wants the

foot and who wants the head?" Jared asked.

Nick thought about horseshoes. He used to play horseshoes on the lawn with Jules and his mom and dad long ago on summer nights. Lassoing a giant couldn't be very different from that. It wasn't really athletic. As long as he could get up the tree.

"I can take the head," said Nick.

"What are we going to do when he's tied up?" Laurie asked. "How are we going to drag him away from here?"

Jared looked over at the construction area. "Maybe one of those lifts?"

"You want to steal a lift?" Nick demanded.

"Okay, what's your genius plan?"

"Shut up, please," Laurie whispered. "We can worry about what to do with the giant later. Taloa's not going to last much longer."

"You're right," Nick said. "Ready?"

"Ready," said Laurie.

"Ready," said Jared.

Nick put his foot on the lowest branch of the oak tree and shoved himself up. The bark was rough under his hands, and he wished that he'd picked throwing the wire over the giant's foot. He hadn't climbed a tree in years, but he couldn't let himself think about failing. With a grunt, he pushed himself higher.

Looking down, he had a dizzy impression of how far he would fall if his foot slipped. He felt cold all over.

By testing the limb twisting in front of him, he'd inched his way close enough that he could smell the giant's mineral breath, which was like freshly dug soil. He felt smaller than a mouse. If he could barely find his way out of a field full of bloated fireflies, he had no idea how he was going to manage this. He looked down and nodded to Laurie anyway.

Holding the knotted circle of wire between them, Laurie and Jared crept to either side of the giant's massive foot. Nick tried not to breathe, conscious of every sound. If it stopped looking at Taloa and looked at its foot right now, it could crush Laurie and Jared like ants.

The nixie's song swelled nervously, as if trying to keep the giant's attention.

Together, Laurie and Jared threw their cord. It went over the giant's foot just like the directions said it should.

Nick's palms went damp with sweat. He lifted his own loop of wire. Somehow, he had to swing it over the giant's head without getting the giant's attention.

Take deep breaths, Nick told himself.

Let out the breath you took, he told himself.

It's just like throwing horseshoes. Horseshoes aren't

Nick's palms went damp with sweat.

*really a sport. You might not be good at sports, but
you're good at horseshoes.*

He concentrated and tossed the wire into the
air. Swung it around. Aimed.

The giant swung toward him, its black eyes
gleaming with reflected light. Nick yelped, but
he didn't hesitate. He closed his eyes and threw
it. The giant bellowed.

Taloa stopped singing.

Nick opened his eyes just in time to see the
giant lunge at him, fists raised. One stone hand
grazed close enough to smash a branch before
the cord pulled tight around the giant's neck.
The enormous creature fell with a sound like
the earth cracking open.

Jared whooped and Laurie yelled—a sound
that seemed more appropriate to terror than to
victory. Nick swung out of the branches, coming
down hard on one knee, scraping the skin.

"Do not for-lo-le-la-get your promise," said Taloa, sinking into the water. *"You are indebted to me."*

"We won't forget," said Laurie.

"We did it," Jared said. "Wow. *Wow.*"

Nick turned to where the giant struggled

against the bonds, kicking and scrambling. Each time it kicked, the wire pulled tighter. With growing horror, Nick realized what the diagram had instructed them to do. The trap was designed to make the giant strangle itself.

"No, wait," Nick shouted, but the giant didn't seem to understand him. It thrashed again, kicking a sheet of water, pounding its head against the ground until it finally went still. Its features relaxed into slackness.

No one cheered. They stared in horror. They'd killed the giant.

A low chuckle from behind Nick made him turn.

"Well, well," said a black man with a huge machete in one sun-leathered and wrinkled

NOSEEUM JACK

hand. He stood just off the road, but he walked toward them. Even in the dim light, the dull metal of the blade gleamed.

The man blinked cloudy eyes and grinned. "Good work, kids. Aren't you gonna finish him off?"

"What?" Nick said. The man actually saw the giant? The man with the giant knife?

"I followed you over from my place. Wanted to see what you were gonna do with the papers you took."

"They were your papers?" Laurie asked.

"We didn't know . . . we didn't know he'd die," said Nick.

"He's not dead," said the man. "Not yet."

"What do you mean?" Laurie asked.

The old man walked up to the giant and shoved his machete through the giant's eye. Its body twitched and then went still. The old man was right—now Nick could see that the giant hadn't been dead before. This stillness was far more terrible. Laurie choked on a sob.

"Now he's dead," said the old man.

"Who are you?" Jared asked. His voice didn't sound very steady.

"Noseeum Jack, they call me," he said. He smoothed back his white hair with one hand. "'Cause I don't see too good anymore. I hunt giants—just like my daddy. You kids aren't half-bad hunters."

Jared swallowed. "Your dad must have been the one writing to my great-great-uncle. Arthur Spiderwick."

Noseeum Jack nodded his head. "Yep. Good man. And good on you for following in his footsteps."

Jared looked embarrassed, but pleased. Nick rolled his eyes.

"So, you *kill* giants?" Laurie asked.

"Yep." He held up his machete. "Stick 'em in the ear. Or the eye, like you saw. Or dynamite. Dynamite works pretty good."

"But can't we just let them go?" she asked, looking over at the body.

"Let them go where? They're territorial, just like us. If we let one giant go, it'll destroy anything it thinks of as on its land." Noseeum Jack shook his head. "You don't understand. I been hunting giants for years, but they've mostly been sleeping giants. You search 'em out, and so long as you're careful, they never wake up. No chance to blow fire or smash things before you get the job done."

"That's terrible!"

"You might think so, but that's because you don't understand. Giants are like cicadas. Just like the cicadas come up all at once every decade or so, giants wake up all at once, too, 'cept they do it every five hundred years," he said. "Good thing you kids showed up when you did."

"Why's that?" asked Nick.

"Me with my sight not being what it used to be, I could use the help. It's time. The giants are all waking up." Noseeum Jack put one wrinkled hand on Nick's shoulder. "And if we don't stop 'em, all of Florida is going to burn."

Nick looked at Jack and Laurie and Jared, then at all the wood frames of half-finished houses in his father's development. He looked over at the lake and the exhausted nixie resting in the mud on the bank. He thought of things, buried things, pushing their way up out of the ground. It seemed to him that no matter how much he wanted to keep things the same, no matter how good he was or what he did or how much he tried to contain, everything was going to change.

And, somehow, he had to change, too.

End of
BOOK ONE

About TONY DiTERLIZZI . . .

Tony DiTerlizzi is the author and illustrator of *Jimmy Zangwow's Out-of-This-World Moon-Pie Adventure,* as well as the Zena Sutherland Award–winning *Ted.* In 2003, his brilliantly cinematic version of Mary Howitt's classic poem "The Spider and the Fly" received stellar reviews, earned Tony his second Zena Sutherland Award, and was honored as a Caldecott Honor Book. His most recent picture book is *G Is for One Gzonk!* In addition, Tony's art has graced the work of such well-known fantasy names as J. R. R. Tolkien, Anne McCaffrey, Peter S. Beagle, and Jane Yolen as well as Wizards of the Coast's *Magic: The Gathering.* He, his wife, and his daughter reside in Amherst, Massachusetts. Visit Tony on the World Wide Web at www.diterlizzi.com.

and HOLLY BLACK

Holly Black's first novel, *Tithe: A Modern Faerie Tale*, was published in the fall of 2002. It was a YALSA Best Book for Young Adults and made YALSA's Teens' Top Ten booklist for 2003. A companion novel, *Valiant: A Modern Tale of Faerie*, won the Andre Norton Award for young adult fiction from the Science Fiction and Fantasy Writers of America. Her most recent solo venture is a *New York Times* bestselling companion to *Tithe* and *Valiant* entitled *Ironside: A Modern Faery's Tale*. She has also contributed to collections by Terry Windling, Ellen Datlow, and Tamora Pierce. Holly also lives in Amherst, Massachusetts. She lives with her husband, Theo, and a remarkable menagerie. Visit Holly on the World Wide Web at www.blackholly.com.

Beware, fair Laurie.
Heed, young Nick. . .

Learn from the tale of
Spiderwick. . . .

NICK VARGAS

The faerie are
a fickle folk.
Be fooled by neither
vow nor joke.

Trust nothing that those tricksters say, and live to trust another day.

LAURIE VARGAS

Give their counsel half an ear, and risk something that you hold dear.

Watch out for giants
in the land.
They slumber just
beneath the sand.

GIANT

And at the hour
of their waking,
strive to help
without forsaking

Nature's steady
ebb and flow—
the circle that you
need to know—

NOSEEUM JACK

because to act in
haste and blindness
only begets woe
and darkness.

Now as rivers
meet the shore,
this tale unwinds
at Neptune's door,

MERMAID

where those who roam
the wat'ry deep
demand a price
both dear and steep—

a prize worth more than
pearls or gold—
"jewels" that can't
be bought or sold

JULIAN VARGAS

but will be seized
till tale is told. . . .

A GIANT PROBLEM
BOOK TWO OF THREE

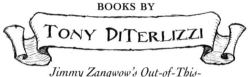
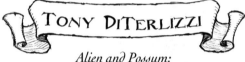

BOOKS BY

TONY DITERLIZZI
AND HOLLY BLACK

ACKNOWLEDGMENTS

Tony and Holly would like to thank
Kevin, our faithful, fantastical guide
for this grand adventure,
Linda, for mapping out Mangrove Hollow
(and the spaghetti!),
Cassie, Cecil, Kelly, and Steve,
for their smarts,
Barry, for all his help,
Ellen, Julie, and all the folks at Gotham,
Scotty and Johnny Lind, for keeping the art on track,
Will and Joey B., for keeping Tony on track,
Theo, for all the patience and encouragement,
Angela (and Sophia) — more Spiderwick!
More endless nights of discussion!
At least it was on a beautiful, sunny Florida beach . . . ,

and all the wonderfully talented folks at S&S for
all of their support in bringing the next chapter
in the Spiderwick tale to life.

The text type for this book is set in Cochin.
The display types are set in Nevins Hand and Rackham.
The illustrations are rendered in pen and ink.
Managing editor: Dorothy Gribbin
Art director: Lizzy Bromley
Production manager: Chava Wolin